THE CHINESE VIOLIN

Text by Madeleine Thien

Illustrations by Joe Chang

Whitecap Books

Vancouver / Toronto

Lin Lin used to play on a
grassy hill in her small village
in China. On Sunday afternoons,
people came from far and wide
with their violins and flutes and
mandolins. Lin Lin and her father
would sit among the butterflies
and birds and flowers and
listen to the music. Lin Lin
loved her small village.

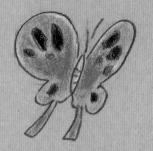

Sometimes, Lin Lin and her father floated the day
away on the river. He would play his violin, and
Lin Lin would try to play it too.

Afterward, she would close her eyes and listen to the sounds—the frogs singing, the children laughing, the drifting cry of the violin.

Lin Lin's father loved their small village too, but he said it was time to leave China. One night, he filled out papers so they could move to Canada. When the papers were approved, he picked Lin Lin up in his arms and lifted her high in the air. Lin Lin pretended to be excited, but in her heart she was frightened.

Before they left, Lin Lin walked through her village one last time. She stood very still and listened to the birds and the flutes, and the wind moving on the grassy hill. The song from a violin drifted toward her. Lin Lin wanted to keep the village in her memory forever.

When they arrived in Vancouver, Lin Lin was surprised by the sounds. Hollering seagulls dipped across the sky. The noises of the cars and people and a new language swept over Lin Lin like an ocean.

At school, the children called to each other in English and played games Lin Lin had never seen before. She stood by herself, listening to their laughter float across the playground. She looked up at the big blue sky, but even the sky felt like a stranger.

Lin Lin's father decided they needed something to lift their spirits. "Lin Lin," he said. "Let's go to the park today. Everyone says the park will make us feel at home again." She followed her father through the city,

through the trees, all the way to the ocean. Lin Lin's
father unwrapped his violin and leaned it against his
knee. When he played the first notes, Lin Lin felt her
heart singing.

Lin Lin fell asleep and dreamed a wonderful dream. She was soaring high in the clouds. When she looked down, she could see her small village and this new city and the deep blue ocean between them. When Lin Lin awoke, her father was playing the violin. The music filled the air

around her. Lin Lin leaned against her father and hoped that one day she would be able to play the violin as beautifully as he did. For the next few weeks, Lin Lin remembered that feeling of soaring among the clouds. School was hard, but the memory comforted her.

One afternoon, she and her father walked downtown. On a busy corner, he unwrapped his violin and leaned it against his knee. He played a beautiful song.

People came and stood in a circle around him. They closed their eyes and listened to the music. When her father finished, they cheered and clapped. They left coins in the cardboard box that Lin Lin had set on the ground.

That evening, Lin Lin and her father set out for home through the meandering streets. She held her father's hand and listened to the coins jingling in the box and the reassuring sound of her father's shoes on the pavement.

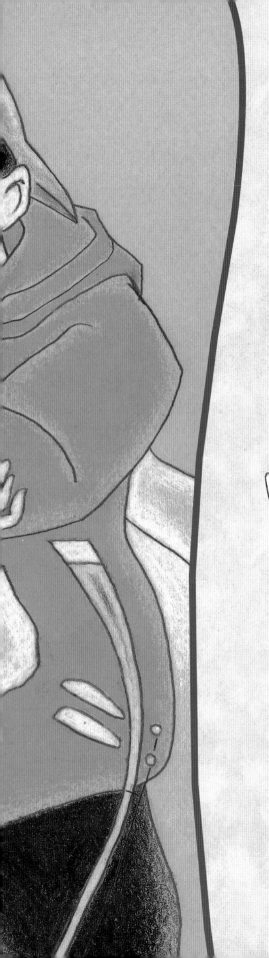

Suddenly, two men came out of the shadows and grabbed Lin Lin's father. She screamed and yelled at them to stop. The men took her father's wallet, and the cardboard box fell to the ground, spilling coins everywhere. The men ran away.

On the sidewalk, Lin Lin's father put his face in his hands and wept. The violin was cracked and broken. Lin Lin wrapped her arms around her father's neck and held him tight.

Over the next few weeks, Lin Lin tried to concentrate on her schoolwork, but her mind was full. She remembered her small village and the music of the violin drifting across the grassy hill. She tried to read her English books, but the words swam in front of her eyes.

All day long, Lin Lin's father worked at his new job. He washed dishes in a busy restaurant.

At night, he helped Lin Lin with her schoolwork. "Don't worry," he told her. "Very soon this place will feel like home."

When Lin Lin saw how hard her father was trying, she didn't want to disappoint him. At school, the teacher helped Lin Lin with her English words. Lin Lin imagined that soon all the words would roll off her tongue and she would be able to laugh and sing alongside the other children.

One day, Lin Lin's father surprised
her with a present. "Lin Lin," he said.
"I know you have been studying very hard.
I have found something special for you."
In his hands was a new violin.

Lin Lin's heart leapt. The violin reminded Lin Lin of her dream. She remembered flying in the clouds, through the big sky. She clutched the violin and jumped into her father's arms.

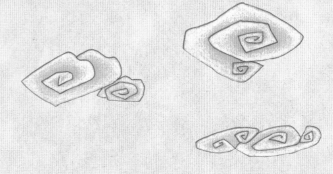

By autumn, Lin Lin could play an
entire song. She practised outside,
beneath the big trees and their tumbling
leaves. One by one, her friends came
to listen. It didn't matter that she was
shy when she spoke. They loved the
sound of her music.

Every time Lin Lin missed her small
village, she played the violin. The music
drifted in the air along with the calling
of the birds and the sound of the wind
in the trees.

One day, in the school auditorium, Lin Lin played the violin for an audience. When she heard the notes, she felt herself soaring with the music, lifted up by all the familiar faces.

In the front row, her father beamed at her.

Lin Lin saw his happy face and heard the sound of her own heart singing.

For my niece, Chenessa Ann Mok. —Madeleine Thien

For my wife, Yang Li, and my sons, Lionel Chang and Daniel Chang, with love. —Joe Chang

Text copyright © 2001 by Madeleine Thien
Illustrations copyright © 2001 by Joe Chang
Whitecap Books
Vancouver / Toronto

Edited by Kathy Evans
Cover and interior design by Tanya Lloyd/Spotlight Designs
Printed and bound in Hong Kong.

NATIONAL LIBRARY OF CANADA CATALOGUING IN PUBLICATION DATA
Thien, Madeleine, 1974–
    The Chinese violin

    ISBN 1-55285-205-9

    1. Chinese—Canada—Juvenile fiction. I. Chang, Joe. II. Title.
PS8589.H449C54 2001   jC813'.6   C2001-910360-3
PZ7.T356Ch 2001

Joe Chang created the story and illustrations for *The Chinese Violin*, originally an animation short for the National Film Board of Canada. This original story, created with images and music, was told without words. In the movement of this story from film to book, Madeleine Thien created the words that would accompany *The Chinese Violin*.

The publisher acknowledges the support of the Canada Council and the Cultural Services Branch of the Government of British Columbia in making this publication possible. We acknowledge the financial support of the Government of Canada through the Book Publishing Industry Development Program for our publishing activities.